DETROIT PUBLIC LIBRARY
3 5674 03684176 6

P9-CFZ-246

by
Robert Munsch

Illustrated by
Michael Martchenko

SCHOLASTIC CANADA LTD.
New York Toronto London Auckland Sydney
Mexico City New Delhi Hong Kong Buenos Aires

The illustrations in this book were painted in watercolor on Arches paper.
The type is set in 20 point Stone Sans.

Published simultaneously in Canada by Scholastic Canada Ltd.

ISBN 0-439-18774-5

Library of Congress Cataloging-in-Publication Data

Munsch, Robert N., 1945-
Zoom! / by Robert Munsch ; illustrated by Michael Martchenko.
p. cm.
Summary: When Lauretta tries out a 92-speed dirt-bike wheelchair, she gets a speeding ticket but also helps out her brother.
ISBN 0-439-18774-5 (POB)
[1. Wheelchairs--Fiction. 2. Speed--Fiction.] I. Martchenko, ill.
II. Title.
PZ7.M927 Zo 2003
[E]--dc21 2002073468

10 9 8 7 6 5 4 3 2 1 03 04 05 06 07
Printed in Canada
First printing, March 2003

For Lauretta Reid, Orillia, Ontario
— R.M.

When her mother came to pick her up at school, Lauretta said, "Look at this ratty old wheelchair! I've had it since forever. I need a new wheelchair!"

"Guess what?" said her mother. "We are getting one today! I wanted it to be a surprise!"

So they went to the wheelchair store to get a nice new wheelchair.

Lauretta's mother said, "How about this? Look at this! A nice new five-speed wheelchair."

Lauretta rode the wheelchair around the store:

ZOOOOOM

ZOOOOOM

ZOOOOOM

and said, "Too slow."

Then Lauretta's mother said, "Well, how about this? Look at this! A nice new ten-speed wheelchair."

Lauretta rode the wheelchair around the store:

ZOOOOOOOOOOM

ZOOOOOOOOOOM

ZOOOOOOOOOOM

and said, "Too slow."

Then Lauretta's mother said, "Well, how about this? Look at this! A nice new 15-speed wheelchair. It's fantastic. It's purple, green, and yellow. It costs lots and lots of money."

Lauretta rode the wheelchair around the store really fast:

ZOOOOOOOOOOOOOOOM

ZOOOOOOOOOOOOOOOM

ZOOOOOOOOOOOOOOOM

and said, "Too slow."

Her mother said, "Well, what sort of wheelchair do you want?"

Lauretta went way in the back of the store and said, "This is what I want. A nice new 92-speed, black, silver, and red, dirt-bike wheelchair."

"Oh, no," said her mother. "It costs *toooo* much money. It goes *toooo* fast. You are *toooo* little for a wheelchair like that."

The lady from the store came over and said, "Take it home for a day. Give it a try for free! See if you like it."

"Wow!" said Lauretta. "We can try it for a day and it will not even cost any money! Pleeeeeeease!"

"Oh, all right," said her mother.

00%
15
15
15
100

When they got home, Lauretta put the wheelchair in first gear and rode up and down the driveway:

ZOOM

But first gear was very slow. So she put it in tenth gear and went:

ZOOOOOOOOOOM

That was still too slow, so she put it into twentieth gear and went really fast:

ZOOOOOOOOOOOOOOOOOOOM

and crashed into her brother.

He said, "Lauretta, if you are going to go so fast, don't go on the driveway. Go on the road."

"Okay, okay, okay!" said Lauretta. "I'll go on the road."

Lauretta went out to the road, put her wheelchair into ninety-second gear and went:

ZOOOOOOOOOOOOOOOOOOOOOOOM

as fast as she could.

A police car came up beside Lauretta. The police officer rolled down the window and yelled, "Hey, kid, pull over! You're speeding."

Lauretta pulled over and the police officer gave her a 100-dollar ticket for speeding. He tied it right to her wrist. Then he said, "Go home, kid! You shouldn't even be on the road at all."

Lauretta went home saying, "Oh, I'm in trouble. Oh, I'm in trouble. Oh, I'm in trouble."

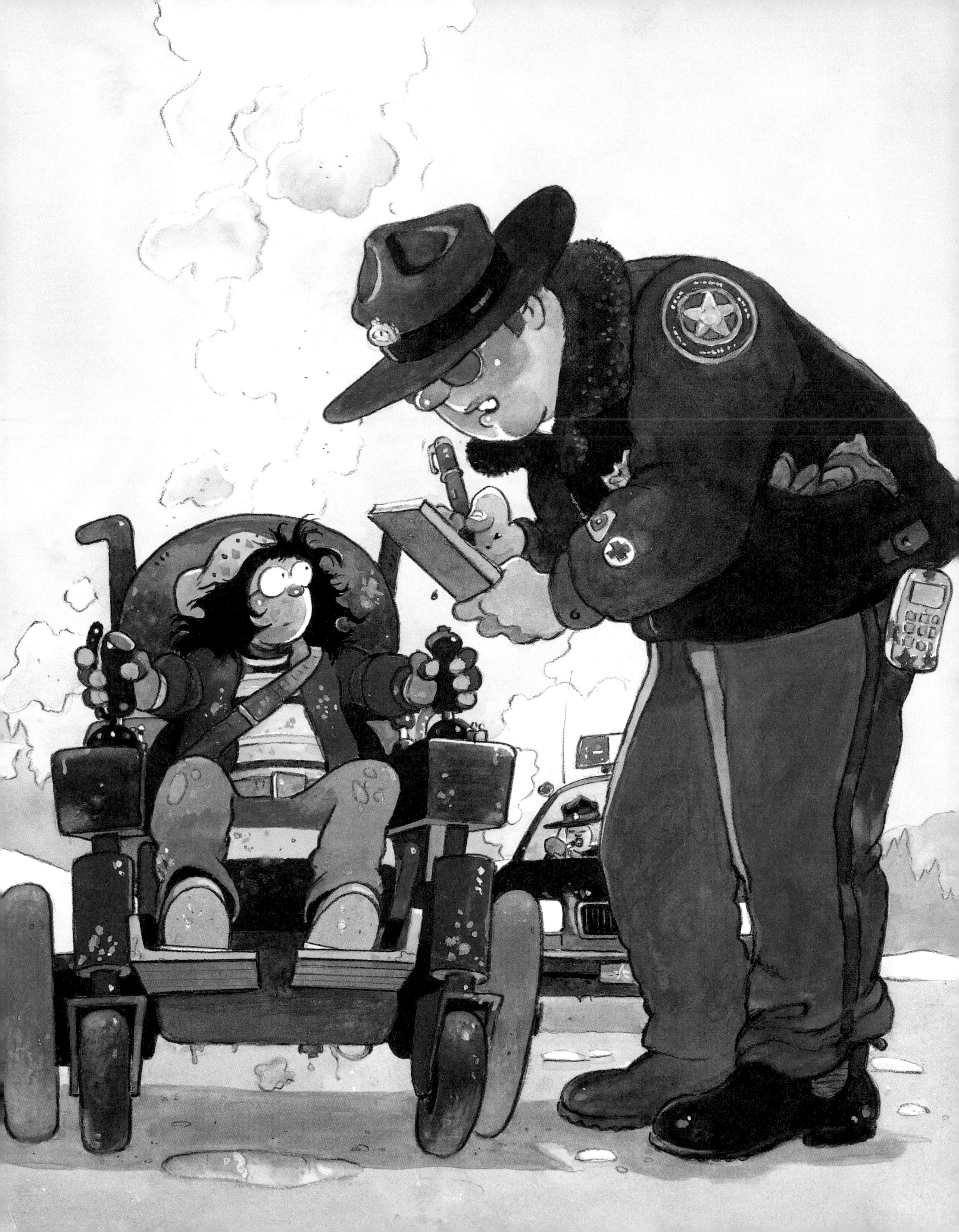

When she got home, her mother said, "Why, Lauretta, what's that on your wrist?"

"It's a ticket," said Lauretta.

"Oh," said her mother. "Is it a ticket to a movie?"

"No," said Lauretta.

"Is it a ticket to a hockey game?"

"No," said Lauretta.

"Is it a ticket to a baseball game?"

"No," said Lauretta. "It's a 100-dollar speeding ticket for speeding in my wheelchair."

"Oh, no!" said her mother. "This is terrible. What will your father say? What will your grandmother say? What will the neighbors say?"

(You know how mothers do that? Well, she did it for a long, long time.)

Finally it was dinnertime.

Lauretta's father said, "That wheelchair is too fast. We are going to have to take it back."

"Yes," said Lauretta's mother. "That wheelchair is too fast. We are going to have to take it back."

Meanwhile, Lauretta's older brother was trying to talk on the phone, argue with Lauretta, feed the dog, and use his fork all at the same time. He stuck the fork right through his finger.

Lauretta's mother yelled, "BLOOD!"

Lauretta's father yelled, "BLOOD!"

Lauretta said, "This house is going crazy."

They all ran out to the car. Lauretta's father turned the key, but the car wouldn't start.

"Oh, no!" yelled Lauretta's mother. "How are we going to get him to the hospital?"

"Don't worry," said Lauretta. "I'll take him in my wheelchair!"

She pulled her brother onto her lap and went down the street in ninety-second gear:

ZOOOOOOOOOOOOOOOOOOOOOOOM

as fast as she could go.

That same police car came up beside her.

Lauretta pointed at her brother and yelled, "BLOOOOOOD!"

So the police car went with Lauretta all the way to the hospital. Lauretta drove in and gave her brother to the doctor, and the doctor sewed up her brother's finger.

Then they went all the way home and knocked on the door:

BLAM, BLAM, BLAM, BLAM

Her mother said, "Oh, Lauretta, you saved your brother!"

Her father said, "You saved your brother! You couldn't have done it without your wheelchair. Lauretta, you can keep the wheelchair."

"Well," said Lauretta, "thank you very much. It's a very nice wheelchair, but I don't want that wheelchair anymore."

"Oh, no," said her mother.

"Oh, no," said her father. "What's the matter with the wheelchair?"

"Well," said Lauretta, "it's

TOO SLOW."

15

416
X2000 +2